CIRCLE OF RETRIBUTION

Future Chron Universe

Volume 6

From The Earth Series

Book 6

D.W. PATTERSON

Fourteenth Printing – May 2023

Cover Image – Courtesy NASA

1

Most predictions of the future had assumed that the first settlement beyond the Asteroid Belt would be a moon of Jupiter, perhaps Callisto. But that didn't happen and as usual, money was the deciding factor. There was no monetary reason to go to any of Jupiter's moons but Saturn's moon, Titan, was interesting and possibly profitable by the early twenty-second-century. Through the mining of valuable Helium 3 (He3) from the atmosphere of Saturn, which the fusion power plants of the Solar System desperately needed, an investment on Titan would return money to the investors in their lifetime.

But even with fusion, the energy was only as cheap as the cost of transporting the fuel that makes that energy. And Mars with its lower gravity and closer proximity to Saturn had at least a factor of ten advantage over Earth when it came to transportation costs. With a population of several million and good governance, the Mars Republic also had the resources, stability and drive to finance the establishment of a Titan base. Earth would gladly pay for the He3 fuel it needed to keep its economies moving and Mars would benefit.

Gardener Abram Jackson had been born in the Asteroid Belt but had spent much of his life on Mars including attending the Mars Space Academy for four years. Gardener had a wiry frame, he was unusually short for an asteroid baby but his height fit his job choice of Aero-SpaceCraft (ASC) pilot. At twenty-five, this would be his first piloting job after graduation and he hoped he was prepared.

Actually, the job to skim Saturn's atmosphere and extract He3 was flown by an autonomous ASC with an Artificial Narrow Intelligence (ANI) system specifically adapted for the mission. Pilots were in effect a backup to the ANI.

"Jackson!" yelled Lt. Macland. The lieutenant was as short as Gardener but had a much stockier build. He also had the requisite crew cut you would expect of a Republic Marine.

"Yes sir!" called Gardener. Although a civilian employee of Titan Enterprises, his flying job made Gardener subject to the military commander responsible for security at the Titan base. The military also maintained the ASCs.

"Jackson, I need you to go over your craft and run a system's diagnostic and generate the necessary reports."

"But sir I've done the diagnostics several times already, and the flight isn't for days, don't you think it's enough?"

"No I don't pilot, now get with it and get me that report or you won't be flying!"

"Yes sir," said Gardener somewhat resentfully.

Gardener headed for the hangar.

Why is the lieutenant riding me so hard? I don't understand it. Maybe he just doesn't like civilians.

Gardener climbed into the ASC1, also known as a "skimmer," which Titan Enterprises of Mars had developed. His skimmer was one of half a dozen in the hangar which included the prototype craft along with military transports and research craft. Of all the vessels in the hangar, the skimmers looked the most futuristic. They were sleeker than the others because they were meant to cut through the dense atmosphere of Titan as well as the upper layers of Saturn's atmosphere. Gardener always had an appreciative look on his face whenever he saw a skimmer.

Inside the skimmer Gardener seated himself in the pilot's seat and began to power up the craft. The diagnostic wouldn't require his input until it was done, unless something amiss was discovered. Gardener would occupy himself by dictating a letter to his parents back on Mars with his personal ANI called an Annie.

Gardener began:

Hi mom and dad. I've gotten used to my new routine here on Titan. I mostly go to briefings and classes on the skimmer's operation or simulations of the mission I will be flying. Right now I'm running a diagnostic on the skimmer by order of Lt. Macland. He seems to not like me for some reason but I'm not particularly bothered, have to be doing something I guess.

Titan is surprising. Although we learned all about it at the MSA I'm surprised at how beautiful it can be. Most of the time it's like living inside a cloud, nothing to see. But then it will clear, at least out to a few kilometers and the pink-orange of the sky will become a brilliant gold almost.

Then there are the rainstorms, if a methane downpour can be called rain. I find them fascinating since, as you know, I've never seen rain in person, only on a video screen. The drops of liquid methane against the clear atrium wall, the flowing rivulets they cause outside, I could watch them fall and merge and flow for hours. But it doesn't last long, no more than fifteen minutes I would guess.

The last time it rained I saw lightning. You can't imagine such a sight without seeing it in person. Then there is the thunder. And then you remember that it is methane out there and very explosive. If not for the fact that there is very little oxygen in the atmosphere of Titan the atmospheric methane would be a real danger. But Titan's atmosphere is mostly nitrogen and fires started by lightning are impossible. Still the lightning is disconcerting and I wonder if the base or one of the flying craft has ever been struck.

Well, I see the diagnostic is almost finished so I guess I'll button this up and send it. Love you both.

Gardener read over the letter and then punched the send button on the touchscreen. The letter would be queued to go by radio transmission next time there was a slot for the base personnel's personal communication. Gardener skimmed the diagnostic report and then sent it to the base ANI which would deliver it to Lt. Macland. Gardener hoped it would be the last diagnostic before the flight but he doubted it.

2

Gardener was deep into the simulated mission, flying the skimmer through the atmosphere of Saturn, mining He3 and hydrogen when the alarms sounded. The simulator was incredibly realistic, many times Gardener had almost forgotten he was in a simulator. The emergency alert brought him back to his duties.

What emergency is the lieutenant throwing at me this time?

Gardener brought up the alert screen. He was warned by the skimmer's ANI that all the weather scout ships were offline.

That's ridiculous, they couldn't all have gone down at the same time.

The scout ships were unmanned aerial vehicles (UAV). ANI piloted, that flew ahead of the skimmer to warn of potential storms or other disturbances that should be avoided.

Gardener knew this was just a setup for the real emergency that Lt. Macland was planning next. Still, he went through the emergency checkoff sheet with the ship's ANI. There weren't any recommended procedures for the loss of all UAVs, but there were procedures for the loss of a lesser number. Gardener directed the ANI to put in place the procedures. Radar at maximum, speed reduced one-third and report to base.

Before he could make the call he heard, “ASC1 this is Lt. Macland in flight control report your status.”

"Flight control status is nominal, have lost weather support escort. Am continuing mining operation at reduced rate."

"Understood ASC1," said Macland. He then nodded to the simulations officer. "Give him the works."

The simulations officer nodded and began talking to the simulations interface. "Simulations mark, increase wind speed, cue vortex system," he looked at Macland who smiled, "and partial failure of flight controls. Engage now."

Gardener immediately noticed a lack of response. The ANI struggled to maintain level flight. Gardener felt a sickening oscillation, the craft was pivoting around the yaw axis, like an office chair that slowly swivels one way and then the other. He also noted an element of pitch was also involved, as the nose rose and fell. And then it got worse.

The wind speed indicator which had been showing a steady twelve-hundred kilometers per hour had jumped to thirteen-hundred and was climbing.

Gardener ceased the He3 mining, he closed all exterior ports to the wind. Then he noticed a definite drift to starboard as if something were pulling the ASC in that direction. He contacted flight control, "Flight, this is ASC1, I am having a problem with vehicle attitude and direction, am taking manual control."

"Gardener you better know what you are doing and you better bring that craft back in one piece!" thundered Lt. Macland on the radio.

"Yes sir."

Gardener took control from the ANI and tried to bring the ASC around to its original course. The controls were slow to respond, he managed to pull the nose back in position but now the craft was beginning to be buffeted by increased side winds. He knew he was close to losing control.

Scanning the long-range radar and satellite readouts he set course for what seemed to be a calmer region of the atmosphere. He then returned flight surface controls to the ANI and engaged the attitude thrusters. The ASC being both an airplane and spaceship had flight surfaces for maneuvering in an atmosphere and thrusters for attitude control in space.

“What's he doing?” asked Macland to no one in particular. “He can't use the thrusters while the ANI is flying with the control surfaces can he?” He looked at the simulations officer who just shrugged.

Gardener carefully applied the thrusters in such a way as to assist the AI with the craft's orientation. By working to keep the nose pointed in the proper direction the craft's ANI started to make progress in the desired direction. It wasn't long until the ASC1 was making good speed for the coordinates that Gardener had entered into navigation. He disengaged the thruster system and engaged the mining system again.

Gardener contacted flight control, “Flight, this is ASC1, have moved mining operations to more opportune area. Mission delay estimated at fifteen minutes, unavoidable due to weather encounter.”

Lt. Macland stormed out of the flight control room.

3

Gardener was sitting in the lounge area reviewing flight data from his latest simulation when Maxine Jordan walked in. Her stride was smooth and measured as she had adjusted to the low gravity of Titan faster than anyone. She was also a skimmer pilot who flew out on the same fusion ship that brought Gardener to Titan. She was about the same height as Gardener although of a stockier build. She kept her hair cut short which made her look more like one of the marines than a civilian pilot. Gardener and Maxine had talked all the way from Mars to Titan about flying and the adventures they were looking forward to on Saturn's moon.

"Hey Gardener I hear you had an interesting simulation," said Maxine.

"Yeah Maxine I did. Why, what did you hear?"

"Nothing except that you almost gave Lt. Macland a stroke."

"Really, well that may explain why he wasn't in flight control when I emerged from the simulator. So he was upset, huh?"

"That's what I hear. What did you do?"

Gardener explained to Maxine what had occurred on his simulated mission.

He finished by saying, "I don't think it was very realistic to lose all my escorts at the same time. They are supposed to be preparing me for likely emergencies, not such far-fetched scenarios."

"Gardener you know Lt. Macland doesn't like you, don't you?"

"Yes, although I have no idea why."

"Well I don't know why either but I can tell you one thing, he wants to wash you out of the program."

"You aren't serious?" asked Gardener surprised.

"That's what I love about you Gardener, you always expect the best of people. But some people are never at their best. And they don't like those who are. I think Lt. Macland dislikes you because you are the pilot he once wanted to be."

"You mean Lt. Macland was in pilot's school?"

"Yep, Mars Marine Flight School and he washed out. From what I hear he didn't respond well under stress. Not even when it was simulated. So he never got the chance to fly a real ship. I think because you are the best pilot here he is obsessed with seeing that you wash out in simulations before you ever get to pilot a mission, just like he did."

"I don't know," said Gardener. "It sounds like a lot of trouble to go to, he knows I could lodge a complaint with the company and we both would be sat down until the truth came out."

"I agree, and he knows that you are the one pilot who wouldn't lodge that complaint. You just take what comes at you and make it work. How do you do it Gardener?"

"Maxine, my family has always had the biggest influence on my life. I have a great-great-uncle who wrote books about personal responsibility. And his writing and his attitude towards life has been passed down now for several generations. When you grow up with that kind of background it becomes second nature."

"What was your uncle's name? Have I ever heard of him?"

"Not likely. His writing was not too popular during his lifetime. People on Earth at that time, or since as a matter of fact, have had no use for his kind of philosophy. And those people who probably would find it motivating, frankly they are already motivated and don't need such instruction. I once heard it expressed this way; 'The power of instruction is seldom of much efficacy except in those happy circumstances where it is almost superfluous.' See, people have developed a mindset long before they are ever formally educated. It comes from the family setting."

"Yeah. And now that the Ems are feeding, clothing and housing those people on Earth they don't need family or family approval. I'm glad I was born and raised on Mars.

"My family wasn't a bunch of philosophers but my dad put it this way whenever I'd ask for something; 'Get it yourself, I ain't always gonna be here to get it for you.'"

"Sounds like he was a philosopher Maxine. The best kind, the one that helps you learn to help yourself."

"I guess so. That's why I like you Gardener you're unpretentious but competent."

"High praise," said Gardener smiling.

"Anyway, when are we going to go flying outside on the surface?"

"I think my suit will be ready tomorrow afternoon, is that a good time for you?"

"Sure," she replied.

4

Excursions on the surface of Titan required a dry suit to keep out the minus one-hundred eighty-degree Celsius temperatures and a bottle of liquid oxygen for the breathing apparatus. The bottle needed little refrigeration in the cold atmosphere. The density of the atmosphere is over four times the Earth's and because Titan's gravity is only one-seventh the Earth's, it is possible that humans can fly over its surface with wings attached to their arms. Others on the base had flown, and Maxine and Gardener were determined to try.

Donning their flight suits and breather masks they stepped into the airlock. In a couple of minutes, the airlock cycled and they stepped out onto the surface of Titan. The "sand" under their feet was like an organic soot, hydrocarbon polymers clumped together with about one-third the density of terrestrial sand. Gardener and Maxine carried their "wings" with them. The wings were airfoils about six feet long and weighing almost nothing on Titan. Gardener himself weighed only about twenty pounds on the Saturn moon.

They started off in the direction of a nearby hill that had been christened "Kitty Hawk" by other fliers. Gardener had drilled one of the other pilots, Lance Germaine, about how to handle the wings. Lance had flown already from Kitty Hawk. He was taller than Gardener by almost four inches with long arms and legs. Gardener wondered how he cramped into the cockpit of his ASC.

"Gardener," said Lance, "figure out the wind direction and run into the wind just like you were piloting a plane. I would glide a couple of times to get a feel for how to balance yourself in the air. Then when you are comfortable with gliding, take off as usual but flap your arms just like a bird on Earth. You can glide back down when you get tired. Just one other thing, make sure you always keep up with the direction of the wind. The airfoils we use for wings don't travel downwind very well."

Gardener had explained what Lance told him to Maxine. When they reached the top of Kitty Hawk, Gardener keyed his mic and asked, "You first or me?"

"You first," said Maxine, "I want to watch you to get an advantage."

"Okay," said Gardener, "here goes."

The flight suit was similar to the old wing-suits used on earth. A web of material between the legs allowed the pilot to run on the ground and use his legs for stabilization when in the air. Another web of material extended from each arm tapering into the body at the waist creating a triangle. The arm material extended as much as two feet beyond the flier's hands. Unlike the old wing-suits, Titan's flight suits had active compensators built-in to help maintain proper flight attitude. This kept the suits from rotating around the fliers yaw axis as was common with wing-suits.

From its top, Kitty Hawk sloped downward in all directions. Gardener consulted the heads-up display of his face mask to note wind direction, the data came from the base weather center through a radio link. Gardener turned and began walking down the slope into the wind. He spread his arms out and sped up his descent. Before long he could feel the pressure of Titan's atmosphere against the suit wings. He started to flap, the airfoil shape of the wings started to lift Gardener into the air. He was no more than a few feet off the ground when he noticed he was climbing at a high rate. Checking the wind speed he was surprised to find it had increased to twenty kilometers per hour. Enough to lift him without any effort on his part.

He tried to adjust his speed of ascent by pulling his arms in to lower the lift of the airfoil. Something happened, his right hand slipped out of the grip glove. The airfoil on that side dipped, the other side rose. Before he could correct he found himself upside down and falling. He pulled his knees up and hit the ground on the back of his heels before rolling the rest of the way down the hill and landing sprawled on his back.

Before he could stand and make an inventory of himself Maxine was bending over him. He could see her yelling something at him from behind her suit mask. He realized that something had happened to his communications module. Maxine bent closer, he didn't need his comm module to hear her.

"What are you doing you idiot, trying to kill yourself!"

He shook his head and motioned for her to help him up. When he finally got to his feet he was surprised to find that he was whole and in one piece until he started to flex his right hand. The fingers on that hand didn't want to flex which was bad enough but the thumb was absolutely immovable and throbbing with pain.

"You okay, can you walk?" yelled Maxine.

He nodded and yelled back, "My radio is out but I'm fine except for my right hand, it's throbbing."

"Let's get you back to base and have the doctor look at that hand."

5

Gardener winced when the doctor took his hand. "You've sprained the ulnar collateral ligament of your right thumb Mr. Jackson," said Dr. Kaye. Dr. Hilton Kaye had come to Titan as chief medical officer for H3 Industries, the conglomeration of companies that provided the private investment for the Titan base. Dr. Kaye was slightly taller than Gardener, still in his thirties and already on his way to becoming rotund.

"What does that mean doctor?"

"It means that the ligament on the inside of your middle thumb joint, the metacarpophalangeal, is strained and that's causing the pain and incapacity."

"What can we do about it?"

"We need to keep your thumb completely immobile for the next three weeks. That means you will have to wear a cast continuously for that amount of time. After that, we will apply a splint that you can take off for rehabilitation exercises but wear at all other times for three more weeks. I expect by then it will be feeling better."

"So you expect a complete recovery?"

"I don't see why not as long as you are careful during rehabilitation to keep that thumb as immobile as possible."

"I will," said Gardener.

"Okay," said Dr. Kaye. "I'll send the nurse in to get that cast started."

After the nurse finished with the cast which was little more than an open mesh that when activated held the thumb rigidly. Gardener left the infirmary and headed for the common area. The main building was arranged around a central igloo-shaped hub which housed the cafeteria as well as administrative offices. Around this hub, there were remote work areas such as the infirmary, similar in shape but smaller. All five of these remote work areas were connected by corridors to the central hub in a starfish pattern. This design had been simpler for the automated three-dimensional printers to weave as they worked to build the base.

Gardener walked carefully along the corridor. A supply robot rolled past on its way to the infirmary.

Because of the low gravity on Titan, it was easy to find yourself moving too fast and bounding too far and high. The corridors and hubs had high ceilings to accommodate but new residents could still hurt themselves until they got used to the change. Gardener had adapted quickly and moved along the corridor effortlessly, like a pro.

He was sitting at a table and trying to open a sugar packet for his coffee when Maxine and Lance walked up.

"A cast," said Maxine. "A cast is going to be a problem with flying the skimmer isn't it?"

“I don't know,” said Gardener. “I think I can work around it, I only have to wear it for three weeks and then just a thumb mesh which will allow more mobility for my fingers.”

Just then Lt. Macland walked into the room.

“Jackson!” yelled Macland, the room got quiet. “I heard that stupid trick you pulled. Why do you think the citizens of Mars paid for your training? So you could sit on your ass drinking coffee in the canteen? Do you have any idea what you've done?”

“Lt. Macland sir, I have a minor injury and I assure you that it will in no way affect my performance. I will be ready to do my job when needed.”

“We'll see about that. You will report to the Captain's office in the morning and tomorrow afternoon you will be in the simulator. I want to know exactly what you can do with that injury. Your first mission payload from Saturn will not be delayed, if you cannot perform to my satisfaction in the simulator tomorrow someone else will fly that mission. Do you understand?”

“Yes sir, Lt. Macland,” Gardener said, seemingly without concern, “I understand.”

Most of the people in the room followed Macland out the door before turning back to Gardener with a look of astonishment.

“Boy that guy is going to get what's coming to him someday,” said Lance. “You aren't the only one he belittles but you do seem to be his favorite. Why is that Gardener?”

"I don't know, some kind of fundamental incompatibility I guess."

The server robot brought Maxine and Lance coffee.

Sipping her coffee Maxine said, "I'll tell you why, because Macland can't and Gardener can, it's as simple as that."

Lance stared at Maxine, Gardener just smiled.

6

Titan is tidally locked to Saturn, meaning that its period of rotation, sixteen days, is the same as its orbital period around Saturn. But the base stuck to a Martian schedule of slightly over twenty-four hours for its day. Since the thick atmosphere usually obscured any markers in the sky this wasn't a hardship for base personnel.

Gardener slept well and was in Captain Winghams' office promptly at nine the next morning, Titan time.

Lt. Macland began, "Captain Wingham if I may."

"Continue," said Wingham.

"As you know Captain, Gardener Jackson is scheduled to fly the first mining mission in two weeks. However, he has now put that mission in jeopardy because of his poor judgment. As you can see he has an injury requiring him to wear a mesh cast on one hand. I believe that this injury will be detrimental to his ability to perform his flight duties."

"Captain if I may," said Gardener.

"Yes Mr. Jackson."

"I admit to poor judgment in my choice of recreation with the flight only a couple of weeks away. However, I believe I can perform up to my full potential even though this cast does restrict my mobility somewhat. And by the time of the mission, I will only need a thumb mesh on my hand which should give me even greater mobility."

"Captain," said Lt. Macland. "I admit it is possible that Mr. Jackson can fly the mission in his present physical condition. We will find that out this afternoon, I've scheduled a simulator session with Mr. Jackson. However, his flight readiness is not in question. What is in question is Mr. Jackson's decision-making ability. His actions show a disregard for the importance and success of this mission. As much as we need an aviator with superior flight skills, we also need an aviator that can make the right decisions under pressure. And that is not a skill that Mr. Jackson has demonstrated recently."

Before Gardener could speak up Captain Wingham began, "Well Lieutenant as I understand it Mr. Jackson's activity that led to his injury is common enough on the base. Surely we should expect some mishaps. And I think that such activity, the chance to stretch your legs outside, is important for maintaining morale. Perhaps we should give Mr. Jackson the benefit of the doubt as far as his decision-making ability. From what I have seen his simulator results are excellent. And I believe you have prepared him quite well for any emergencies. I commend you on your efforts."

Lt. Macland stuttered, "I, I have always tried to prepare all the pilots to the best of my ability sir. I wouldn't do any less, our mission is quite important to me. That is why Mr. Jackson's recent actions are of concern..."

“I understand Lieutenant but why don't we wait and see how Mr. Jackson handles the afternoon simulation you have prepared for him. We can discuss any further actions necessary afterwards.”

“Yes sir,” said Lt. Macland.

“Thank you sir,” said Gardener.

Gardener and Macland rose to leave the room meeting at the door. “I'll see you this afternoon Mr. Jackson,” snarled the Lieutenant.

“Of course Lieutenant.”

7

Gardener arrived for his afternoon flight simulation on time. He was surprised to see all those in attendance. Of course, he expected Captain Wingham might show up but he didn't expect to see most of the other pilots including Maxine and Lance. They stood against the back wall trying to remain out of sight and mind. Both nodded to him when he entered the room.

Gardener was a bit disconcerted until he took his seat in the simulator. Then his mind focused and it was as if he were home. He felt so comfortable that he almost fell asleep while the technicians readied the simulator.

"Mr. Jackson," he heard Lt. Macland call.

"Yes Lieutenant," said Jackson.

"Are you ready?"

"Ready when you are Lieutenant."

"Flight simulation oh nine five three two, pilot Jackson ready, begin when ready flight."

Gardener focused on the controls, his breathing was relaxed. "ASC1 this is flight control, you are cleared for takeoff."

Gardener's screens came alive. Looking out from the simulator it seemed he was aligned on the runway outside Titan base. He began his pre-roll procedures. "Roger, flight control. Beginning pre-roll."

Take-off was flawless and he climbed immediately. He allowed the ANI to take over and it wasn't long until the skimmer was in the upper atmosphere of Titan.

"Flight control this is ASC1, I am about to begin trans-Saturn orbital lock. Nuclear-thermal rockets nominal, flight system nominal, guidance nominal, beginning orbital insertion, now."

The nuclear-thermals kicked, or that's what Gardener called it each time he engaged them and broke free of the atmosphere of Titan. The ASC1's viewing screens showed the blackness of space and the majesty of Saturn. He was now on his way to a rendezvous with the upper atmosphere of that planet.

Here the simulation would skip the cruise phase of the mission and forward to Saturn orbital injection. In this way, all major mission goals were simulated but the relatively quiet times between these markers would be cut out.

"ASC1 this is flight control, Titan escape velocity achieved ready to move to Saturn orbital injection."

"Roger flight control."

The mission continued without incident. Major mission goals were simulated and Gardener completed the mining with a full load of He3 for transport.

"ASC1 this is flight control, prepare for trans-Titan orbital insertion."

"Roger flight control. Ready when you are."

Gardener relaxed momentarily and turned to get his thermos. As he turned his thumb mesh caught on the toggle switch controlling the storage tanks. Before Gardener could react a dump of the He3 tanks began. Because it was an emergency procedure the tanks were half empty before Gardener could cycle the system.

Before he could key his mic, flight control called, it was Lt. Macland. "ASC1, we have an indication of a He3 dump ongoing. Can you advise?"

"Flight control I accidentally caught the tank dump switch as I turned in my seat. I have recycled system, estimate a loss of half He3 resource."

"Okay ASC1 I am calling off further simulation," said Lt. Macland. "Report to the Captain's office for post-mission debriefing. That is all."

Although Gardener was brief in shutting down the simulator when he emerged the room was empty except for the simulation officer who only nodded.

"Please sit down Mr. Jackson," said Captain Wingham.

Gardener took the seat next to Lt. Macland in front of the Captain's desk.

"Mr. Jackson I think that after your simulation today we need to discuss our mission priorities. It appears to me that your injury does have an impact on your ability to carry out the mission. I believe it may be best if we changed the flight assignments. In this way, you will have more time to fully recover."

"But Captain Wingham, what happened in the simulation today could happen to anyone, even without a cast on their thumb. I believe I've discovered an ergonomic design flaw in the cockpit design. We should look into redesigning that switch so that it is not as easy to trip accidentally."

Lt. Macland spoke up, "Mr. Jackson I think that you are not listening. We have given you a fair chance to show your capabilities within the limitations of your injury and you have shown us less than ideal performance. Blaming your simulation failure on cockpit design is disingenuous to say the least. And at the worse it seems like a personality flaw, failing to take responsibility, something I believe I brought up before. You know we still use mechanical switches for the very reason that you are disparaging them, they take a physical action on the part of the pilot to actuate, unlike touchscreen controls which are much easier to accidentally engage."

"I know that Lt. Macland. However, I think that toggle is in the wrong place. The mechanism should be moved or the actuator changed to perhaps a push-button to prevent accidental engagement. At least a flight warning should be issued regardless of what happens to me."

"Mr. Jackson," said the Captain. "I can assure you that a flight warning will be issued about that toggle switch. And your reassignment will not affect your future here. But we must error on the side of caution. You will not be making the first mission flight or any flight until that cast and subsequent splint comes off, do you understand me?"

"Yes sir, thank you sir." Gardener rose to leave.

"I told you, so arrogant," he heard Lt. Macland say as Gardener was closing the office door.

8

Gardener began a letter to his parents:

Hi, mom and dad. I've had a little setback here. I told you about my injury last time and that I didn't think it all that serious physically but unfortunately it has had some serious consequences for the mission.

I had a problem in the simulator the other day. I accidentally tripped the emergency tank dump toggle switch and lost about half of the He3 load I had just mined. The mesh cast caught on the toggle as I turned in my chair. Although the cast probably caused my thumb to hang lower than it usually does I think the emergency toggle is in a bad location and it could have happened to anyone, cast or not.

But the Captain and Lieutenant didn't agree with me so I've been grounded until my thumb heals. I think it was probably prudent on the part of the Captain to do so but I still urged him to redesign that toggle so that it couldn't happen again. They only agreed to issue a flight warning so we'll see.

It does bother me some that Lt. Macland seems so hostile to me. I heard him call me arrogant as I was leaving the Captain's office. I think he confuses arrogance with confidence, you have to believe you can do the job don't you? Anyway, I wish he and I could work more together rather than at cross purposes.

So I haven't much to do for a while. They haven't assigned me to another flight yet and the second flight won't be for several weeks after the first as the first will be reviewed quite extensively before another mining run is made.

I'm disappointed but not depressed, I'll get my chance. Meanwhile, I hope to be of some help to whoever gets the first flight assignment. - Love, Gardener.

Gardener sent his mail and turned off his Annie and folded it for storage in his flight jacket pocket. It had been a long day and he went to bed early. He thought for a while about what he could have done differently in the simulation but decided that it was just an accident not a glaring deficiency in his training or skill-set. He went to sleep.

Maxine wasn't at breakfast as usual, the following morning. She showed up fifteen minutes late.

"Hey Maxine what kept you?" asked Gardener.

"Did you oversleep?" asked Justin Tor, another one of the ASC pilots, with a smile.

"No I didn't oversleep Justin. I've never overslept in my life. I had a message to report to Captain Wingham's office first thing this morning, that's why I'm late."

"So what did the Captain want?" asked Lance.

"He, well he gave me the maiden flight assignment," she said looking at Gardener. "Sorry Gardener."

"No, Maxine that's great," said Gardener. "If I can help you in any way let me know."

"Thanks Gardener. I was worried you might be upset. I could use your help to get up to speed fast since the flight is scheduled two weeks from now."

"Really," said Justin. "They've finally made up their minds. Of course, we get short notice as always."

"Don't worry Maxine, I'll give you all the help you'll need," said Gardener.

He continued, “Justin, I don't think they deliberately keep us in the dark, I don't think they know themselves. A lot of people, including some not on Titan, have an input into the scheduling. First and foremost, Titan Industries, our employer as we all should remember.”

Justin just shrugged.

Lance added, “It doesn't matter. At least one of us is going soon. That means the rest of us will have a chance not long afterwards.”

9

Maxine's flight went flawlessly. So did Lance's and Justin's. The mined He3 had made its way back to Mars and had been transshipped to Earth. The corporation was making a profit from its investment for the first time. Everyone was in a good mood, even Lt. Macland, but he knew something the pilots didn't.

Gardener was summoned to the Lieutenant's office.

"Sit down Jackson," said Lt. Macland pleasantly. "I have something to tell you. As you know the other pilot's flights have all been nominal, I would say they have been perfect wouldn't you?"

"Yes sir," said Gardener. "They are all excellent pilots."

"Good, the corporate board has decided, with the acquiescence of Captain Wingham I might say, that the next pilot to fly will be Maxine followed by Lance, Justin and then Maxine again."

Gardener felt his heart jump.

"You see they have been so pleased with the way things are going that they want to hold you in reserve in case any of the other pilots have an injury or becomes too sick to fly their next mission," he smiled. "Do you have any questions?"

"Just one. Did you agree with this decision Lieutenant?"

"Yes I did Jackson, you see it was my suggestion."

“I see, Lieutenant would you do me a favor?”

“Okay, I guess so,” said Macland hesitantly.

“Would you informally tell the Captain and Titan Industries that I will not be renewing my contract when this one is up. I will make an official declaration as we get closer to the end of the contract period. They may want to see about getting my replacement ready before I leave.”

“Oh I would be pleased to inform them of your decision Gardener, you can count on me,” said Lt. Macland smiling broadly.

Gardener had left Lt. Macland's office and was sitting in his quarters dictating a letter to his parents when the door alarmed. It was Maxine.

“Hey Gardener, what's up, I thought you might want to get some dinner.”

“Hi Maxine, I'm just finishing my letter to my parents letting them know I'll be home soon.”

“What do you mean, you'll be home soon?”

“I had a meeting with Lt. Macland.”

“Great, another meeting with Macland.”

Gardener smiled, “Yes and he has informed me that I am on permanent reserve status for the rest of my contract. The only way I will fly a mission is if you or Lance or Justin can't fly. So I told Lt. Macland that I would not be renewing my contract with the company when it expires."

"Sounds like politics to me. I didn't think Macland would stoop so low. He was behind it wasn't he?"

"Yes, he said he initiated the change."

"I thought so. He's been trying for a long time to get you Gardener, and now he's done it. I hope you know you're playing right into his plans."

"I understand what you are saying Maxine but I'm not interested in playing politics, as you put it, with Lt. Macland. I want to pilot a ship. If I can't do that here I'll do it somewhere else."

"You might. If Macland doesn't spread the rumor that you quit. Which I'm sure he will if he gets the chance. Remember, ASC pilots are a small fraternity, news gets around, especially if it's bad news."

"You think Lt. Macland will keep pursuing some kind of vendetta against me even when I leave here?" asked Gardener incredulously.

"The Macland I know will do just that."

"Maybe it's time I tried to find out just why Lt. Macland treats me this way. I know you think he's jealous, but jealously usually ends when one party wins."

"You're right. I know what I said but his latest actions seem more premeditated than I expected. You should find out what exactly is bugging him about you."

Gardener shook his head, "Maybe you're right, I'll ask my dad to look into the Lieutenant's past and see if there is any reason he should show such malice towards me."

10

The accident happened quickly. One minute Justin was in complete control of ASC3 and the next minute it was spinning almost uncontrollably. Later after the investigation was complete it became apparent that it was as much due to luck as to skill that he made it back in one piece.

Justin hadn't remembered much after the spin began because he was thrown from the pilot's seat and hit his head. Before blacking out he was able to enter the emergency protocol which righted the ship and sent it on a trajectory for Titan with him unconscious. The ship brought him back to the vicinity of Titan where the pilot's cage separated and served as an escape module. He was rescued by a military hopper, a conventional rocket-powered ship that could make short hops along the surface of Titan and refuel *in situ* if necessary. The remainder of ASC3 was lost.

Lt. Macland was in Capt. Wingham's office reviewing the situation.

"And the doctor says that pilot Tor will be sidelined for how long?" asked the Captain.

"The doctor believes it will be a couple of months before Tor will fly sir," said Lt. Macland.

"Okay then we are going to need a pilot, do you think Jackson is up to it?"

"He would be my last choice sir."

"He is our last choice Lieutenant," said the Captain somewhat irritated. "Do you think he can fly?"

"I don't know sir. I haven't seen Pilot Jackson in simulation since the incident."

"Very well Lieutenant since you obviously don't want to make this decision I will make it. Get out of here and send Jackson in."

Gardener was visiting Justin in the infirmary when Lt. Macland's adjunct found him. "The Captain wants to see you right away pilot."

Gardener settled into the seat across the desk from Captain Wingham.

"Good to see you Gardener," said Captain Wingham. "As you know we've had a mishap with ASC3. The ship is a total loss but fortunately, the pilot, while injured, made it back. But the doctor tells me he will miss his next scheduled flight. That's where you come in. What I want to know is if you feel up to taking a turn in the rotation?"

"Yes sir," said Gardener. "I haven't practiced in a while as you probably know, but I think I could be up to speed by the time Justin's turn comes around. That would be about six weeks wouldn't it?"

"Yes Justin's next scheduled flight was in six weeks but I'm not talking about you taking that flight, I want you to take the next flight."

"In two weeks," exclaimed Gardener.

"Yes, in two weeks. You see if you take the next flight you can still leave as scheduled. And if you take the next flight then by the time Pilot Tor's flight assignment comes around again either he will be healthy or his replacement will have arrived. So it works out best for all of us if you are up for the next scheduled flight which I believe would have been Pilot Jordan's."

"I see," said Gardener, he paused a moment. "Yes Captain I'm up for it. I believe I'm still sharp enough for flying and there's plenty of time for a few simulations to refresh my skills if needed."

"Excellent Pilot Jackson. I think this will be a benefit to all of us. And thank you for your willingness to work with me. I was afraid you might have been shall we say, soured on the whole experience."

"Flying is flying, and for that, I'm always ready sir."

11

Gardener had practiced a couple of simulations. He hadn't been rusty at all. Since it would have been Maxine's flight she was there to help. Even Lance came by. But surprisingly Lt. Macland did not show up even though he was the officer in charge of simulations.

After his last practice, Maxine remarked on the Lieutenant's absence. "I wonder where Lt. Macland has been keeping himself. I've never seen or heard of a simulation run that he didn't watch over."

"I don't know," said Gardener. "But with or without him I think I'm ready for my flight. At least I had you to help me Maxine, thanks."

"You're welcome Gardener, I haven't forgotten that you did the same thing for me when I was in your situation."

"Well the flight is early tomorrow. I'm going to have a light dinner in my room and mail mom and dad. Will I see you in the morning Maxine?"

"Sure, get plenty of rest, it's a long ride."

Gardener ate his dinner and finished the letter early. He laid down to go to sleep. But unusually, he didn't go right to sleep. He thought about the flight. He thought about his mom and dad. He wondered where Lt. Macland had been the last two weeks. He thought about Saturn waiting for him, beautiful but dangerous. He was wondering about what the Saturn weather report would be when he drifted off to sleep.

Lt. Macland had finally reappeared. He was in the flight control room as Gardener was going through final flight checks.

This take-off would be a little different from the simulator. The ASCs were hybrid ships. Jet motors would power the takeoff and climb to the top of the main haze layer. At that point, the nuclear-thermal rockets would kick in and kick was the correct word. The ASC would leave Titan's atmosphere at several hundred kilometers and if all went well be on its way to a trans-Saturn insertion orbit.

Gardener's job was to get ASC1 off the ground and into the atmosphere where the ANI would take over with Gardener monitoring.

"Flight this is ASC1. Pre-flight checklist nominal, preparing for roll."

"Roger ASC1, clear for roll."

Gardener lifted the ASC into the air flawlessly. He was passing through ten kilometers in altitude when he heard flight control calling.

"ASC1 this is flight control, we monitor you have not passed control to the ANI, is that correct?"

"ASC1 to flight, passing control now." Gardener had been so excited about actually flying again that he had forgotten to pass control to the ANI as required in the flight manual. He reluctantly did so.

From here to almost one hundred kilometers he would just be along for the ride. At one hundred kilometers the ASC would be above the main haze layer and most of the atmosphere of Titan and it would be time to switch from jets to the nuclear-thermals. It would take less than five minutes to reach the switch-over point at the skimmer's rate of climb.

Gardner made sure the ANI switched to the nuclear-thermal rocket at the exact moment prescribed in the flight manual. He felt the kick for real this time as the rocket began its burn. The ANI positioned the ASC1 almost vertical.

“ASC1 you are go for trans-Saturn insertion, over.”

“Roger flight control, go for trans-Saturn insertion.”

The drop to Saturn would take about three days as the ASC would be under power all the time.

About the time it took to first reach the Earth's moon.

Gardener wouldn't have much to do until the time came to place the ASC1 into flight position in the upper atmosphere of Saturn. Until then he would sleep, eat and monitor the automatic guidance system. As far as entertaining himself he would have to be satisfied with Maxine's choices. No one, not even Gardener, had thought about changing out the personalized entertainment choices.

12

Who would have thought Maxine liked such mushy movies, thought Gardener. After three days of watching Maxine's video library Gardener was ready for the excitement of orbital insertion at Saturn even though it would be handled by the ANI.

He could see the tops of Saturn's cloud layers as the ASC1 pitched over to retrofire the nuclear-thermal rocket. Then he felt the g-forces as the rocket decelerated the ship into a high parking orbit. The ship soon fired another short burn to lower the ASC1 from the parking orbit to the top of Saturn's atmosphere. The ship then pitched back again. The needed adjustment in velocity would now be handled by methane-oxygen retro-rockets because the ship would be "flying" into a denser and denser atmospheric soup and would need to present its streamlined silhouette to the increasing winds.

Once in the denser atmosphere (though denser is a relative term, it was still quite empty) of Saturn Gardener could see the flight surfaces come to life from watching the instrument readings. He could now begin the mining operations.

Gardener informed flight control that mining operations had begun. He got an affirmative about eight seconds later owing to the round-trip time delay for the radio waves to cover the millions of kilometers between Saturn and Titan.

There wasn't much to do now but monitor the He3 accumulation. Gardener decided to give it an hour before checking. Back after using the zero-gravity shower facility

Gardener checked on the load of He3. He requested the ANI to estimate the time to full load. Four days was the answer. Not a bad time range but not good either.

Gardener requested from flight control the approval that he take the ASC1 lower to increase the rate of He3 harvesting. Flight approved. Gardener commanded the ASC1 to lower its altitude.

Other ASC flights had flown lower for the same reason but Gardener knew that there was danger in taking the ship too low. Too low and the energy required to escape the atmospheric drag would become too great. The ANI on board was programmed to warn Gardener when he was about to breach the limits of operability but no one had ever reached that limit so the accuracy of the warning had never been tested.

Deeper in Saturn's atmosphere the accumulation rate of He3 increased to a level that was acceptable to Gardener. He would be finished mining in two days instead of four. Gardener relayed the information to flight control. A slight buffeting was the only clue that the ship had gone deeper into the atmosphere.

Gardener settled in for his duty as the ship's babysitter, it would handle the routine chores of mining the He3. The ship would call Gardener if it encountered a situation it couldn't handle. Otherwise, Gardener was free to do as he wished until the mining operation was over. Gardener didn't wish to watch any more of Maxine's movies so he settled for reading and working on a letter to his parents. Gardener informed his parents that he was in orbit around Saturn on a mining mission and everything was going fine. He asked if they had discovered anything about the issue he had written of in his last letter.

It was later that evening when Gardener received a letter in reply from his parents.

Dear Son. Your mother and I were so pleased to hear from you and that your mission is going well. We hope everything goes as planned and that you have a complete success.

Concerning that issue, you asked about. We have discovered something that may be of interest to you. The party you asked about is in a remote way linked to our family. As best we can tell the party of interest had an ancestor that crossed paths with one of your ancestors a few decades ago. We suggest you look up an incident that occurred around that time with a UN ship called the Amity and your great-grandfather. Pay particular attention to what happened to the Captain of that ship after the incident and you will know why his descendant, the person you asked us about, might display such an attitude towards you.

Good luck son, hope to see you soon. - Mom and Dad.

Gardener looked over the letter again. Something involving an incident with grandpa Martin. What could that be, wondered Gardener. He knew that his grandpa had helped open up the Asteroid Belt for mining, Martin even ended up being the miner's representative on Mars. Well, he had another day and a half to find out and not much else to do.

Because of the communication satellites now in Saturn orbit Gardener could do his research almost uninterrupted. He found the connection between his family and Lt. Macland's family later in the evening. It seemed that Macland's grandfather on his mother's side and Gardener's grandfather, Martin, had crossed paths on an obscure asteroid.

Macland's ancestor was captain of the UN ship *Amity* when Gardener's grandpa Martin was just a young graduate of the Mars Academy. Martin had gone to the Asteroid Belt to warn the fledgling miners of the efforts of the UN to interfere with their mining claims. The UN ship had come to claim the Asteroid Belt for commercial interests but in the guise of humanity in general.

Martin and the miners had opposed the crew of the *Amity* and the ship had failed in its mission. The captain of the *Amity*, Lt. Macland's maternal grandfather, had his career cut short because of the failure. The family lost it's influence and wealth soon thereafter. The old captain had always blamed Martin.

So that was the connection. If Lt. Macland had heard these complaints repeatedly as he grew up perhaps he would hold resentment towards the descendants of Martin wherever he found them. Perhaps that was why Macland was always riding me and making my life difficult.

Okay, I think I understand what's been going on, but for now, I have a mission to accomplish and I need to get some rest.

13

Gardener woke to alarms. He floated out of his bunk and quickly propelled himself the few feet to the flight deck. At first, it was hard to grasp the many alarms. Every system in the ship seemed to be in crisis. But Gardener took a deep breath and focused on first things.

And the first thing he was concerned with was the ship's flight status. He immediately canceled the audible alarms so he could concentrate. Focusing only on the flight systems Gardener soon discovered that the skimmer was in perfect trim. Mining operations had suspended automatically, Gardener had no idea why. However, he could see that he had almost a full load of He3.

He next checked life support, navigation, external sensor nets and other systems. All were in alarm but none seemed to be outside normal operating parameters. None of the alarms would clear either. Gardener could think of only one way to get control of the situation, a system reboot.

He keyed in the reboot code and waited. The ANI restarted, each system coming online in nominal condition. Finally, the displays cleared and everything seemed back to normal, except.

Except for the system memory which showed an absence of data. The memory had been wiped clean. Gardener wasn't sure if it occurred during the reboot or before, he hadn't thought to run the diagnostics with all the distraction from the alarms. But now he set about to systematically run through all the diagnostics in the system.

It was a few minutes before he got the results and felt a first twinge of fear. All the diagnostics showed a loss of mission information. There were no navigational coordinates, no flight history before the reboot, no communications parameters, nothing in the system that could be used to fly the ship. Gardener was surprised that such a complete loss of data could happen. He knew he would need to restore all the systems. That was when he got his second twinge of fear.

The system refused to restore and when Gardener ran memory diagnostics it showed that there wasn't any data in the backup memory to restore.

"Impossible," Gardener said aloud.

There was no re-initialization then, there was no restoring navigational coordinates, no restoring the flight plan, no communications because the radio was software-based, the ANI would work but it would not be able to take the ship to Titan without the flight plan, everything would have to be entered manually now. He tried the comm anyway, no response.

No one has ever flown one of these in space without navigational automation. No one has ever even flown one out of the atmosphere of Saturn.

He closed his eyes a moment.

Well I guess I will have to unless I can restore the data lost.

The flying characteristics of the ASC were solid. The ship would trim itself with input from the ANI or human pilot if needed. As long as it was set up in the proper orientation it was a dream to fly. Gardener felt good about his chances.

He glanced at the instrument panel. I've got all the flight instruments necessary, he thought. The vertical speed and attitude indicator were the primary readouts needed, they seemed to be working fine. He looked around himself at the rest of the cockpit. He got up and got his helmet, attached the breather and strapped himself tightly to the pilot's seat, just in case. He took the flight controls.

The ASC1 responded deftly. Gardener set the ship up for a slow climb. It would take some time to reach the upper atmosphere where the nuclear-thermal rocket could fire with full thrust. Then Gardener would be in orbit but essentially lost as to the location of Titan. He would have to figure out how to navigate without the benefit of automation or communications.

The more Gardener thought about it the more he realized that he had no chance to recreate the trajectory he needed without the computer memory. Even the inertial navigational system memory had been lost. Had it been available he would have at least have had a chance to recreate the trajectory needed. The inertial system recorded the complete mission trajectory basically by knowing the set-point (Titan) and using gyroscopes and accelerometers to track the subsequent path. The programs necessary for such calculations were still in the non-volatile memory, they just needed the raw data and time to do the calculations.

Just the raw data, that's all I need.

Then it occurred to him. His Annie had all the necessary sensors built in. It had a positioning system that could provide the set-point. It would have been logging the sensor data from the start of the mission, even before. The only question, was it still powered and did it have enough memory to hold all that data?

Gardener unbuckled and pushed off to his bunk. There he took the Annie from its velcro hold-down and brought up the navigation app. It was still running. He stopped it immediately. He wanted as much of the initial navigation data as possible, he didn't care about the most recent flight data. The original trajectory, especially Titan departure to Saturn orbit insertion was the important thing. If he had that he could find his way back to the base.

14

Gardener mated his Annie to the ship's ANI system. He downloaded the sensor data, he started the navigation program that would turn the data into a flight trajectory. The program estimated twenty-five minutes until conclusion. Gardener was hungry, he would snack while he waited for the program to finish.

After his snack, he studied the results graphically. The flight path he had been following was clearly shown. The only problem was the data ran out before Titan was achieved. The Annie had started overwriting the oldest data when memory space was needed. Still, it was good enough to get the ASC1 out of Saturn's atmosphere and onto a trajectory that should bring it close to Titan. Gardener now set the program to reverse the trajectory and provide the orbital parameters he would need to create a flight plan, especially the needed velocity to leave Saturn orbit for a transfer orbit to Titan. A transfer orbit would take longer than a powered rendezvous but it was simpler to calculate and implement.

Once the ANI had finished its calculations Gardener had about an hour to get to orbital altitude where he could fire the rocket and enter transfer to Titan. The ANI would conduct the firing sequence, Gardener could relax, maybe for the first time since he noticed the ship alarms.

The interval gave him time to think about how this latest problem fit in with his problems with Lt. Macland.

The chance that the memory loss occurred randomly is slim to none. Too many backup systems had to fail to let such a thing happen. Could Lt. Macland have engineered such a failure?

Gardener didn't know, he didn't think Macland had such capability but he couldn't be sure.

If I get back... When I get back. I'll have to investigate the connection.

The ANI start-up of the nuclear-thermal rocket went flawlessly. It would take three times longer to get back since a transfer orbit was unpowered. Nine days was a long time but supplies were adequate if carefully handled and Gardener knew he should be able to get back to Titan, or at least in its vicinity. Just enough time for a rest and maybe finish watching the rest of Maxine's awful vids.

Normally he would have loaded his Annie with his own video library but he was too busy preparing for the mission. If he had loaded his entertainment it might have taken the memory the data logger needed and Gardener would have no way to get home. All of which made Maxine's videos seem better than before.

Nine days later the last of the vids ended and the transfer orbit was almost complete when Gardener began visually scanning for Titan. He found it easily and took the needed bearings so that the ANI could fly the ASC to it.

Once in orbit around Titan finding the base would be a challenge without radio contact. He was wishing he could reboot the radio software and call base when he realized that the radio hardware itself was undamaged. He could switch it on and it would provide a signal, unmodulated and without intelligence, but a signal that could be tracked by the satellite network orbiting Titan. And that would allow base rescue to find him even if he couldn't find them.

Gardener switched on the radio transmitter and waited. He monitored the ANI insertion of the ASC1 into orbit around Titan. From there the orbit would be lowered until he would be flying the ASC1 in Titan's atmosphere again.

The switch from rocket to scramjet was made and Gardener took over the controls from the ANI. He would fly the ASC1 below sub-sonic speed where the jet engine could be started up. From there he would circle Titan, careful to maintain a minimum altitude above the highest elevations, just in case, until he found the base or base personnel found him.

After a couple of hours and sixteen hundred kilometers, Gardener was feeling very sleepy. He was just about to put the ASC1 under ANI control again when a flash off to his right caught his eye. It was the search beacon of an ASC craft. He flew the ASC1 closer until Gardener could see the pilot's face. With the visor up Gardener could see the big smile on Maxine's face. Using hand signals she indicated for Gardener to follow her and she banked sharply. Gardener was right behind.

15

The debriefing took days. The technicians couldn't explain the memory failure. They called it an unexplained anomaly. Maxine called it sabotage. And Lt. Macland, well the Lieutenant had requested a transfer of duty and had left on the ship that Gardener was supposed to leave on. He had taken Gardener's seat.

Gardener sat down in the Captain's office for his final interview.

"Gardener," began the Captain. "I don't have to tell you how impressed everyone is with the way you handled that mission. Your decision making capability under such stress was remarkable. And the fact that you brought back a full load after facing such adversity has earned you the respect of the corporate board. They have empowered me to offer you whatever you want to stay on with the company. Either here as a pilot or back on Mars as an instructor for our ASC pilot's school. Would you consider such an offer?"

"Captain, I have to be honest with you. I think the Corporation has failed in its due diligence to protect the pilots and others in their employ. I believe they did not do an adequate job of vetting certain personnel. And that has exposed us all to great dangers."

"Now Gardener, I understand your bitterness in this situation but I assure you that the Corporation and it's employees and for that matter, the adjunct nature of my service here has all been carefully considered. We both know who you suspect, who you think caused this situation but I can tell you the flight techs that went over your ship had no other goal than to find out what happened. They have personally expressed their concern that nothing was found and they have gone out of their way to implement further safety measures to protect the ASC fleet even further. I ask you that you not judge the whole organization on what one rogue agent may or may not have done."

"Okay Captain I won't, but let me ask you just one thing. What is going to happen with Lt. Macland?"

"Okay Gardener I am going to tell you something that I'm not supposed to. I do ask that you not repeat what I am about to say."

Gardener nodded OK.

"Lt. Macland is not going to be formally charged with any wrongdoing. He is going to be allowed to resign his commission voluntarily. If he does not resign his commission he is going to serve the remainder of his enlistment on a communication relay asteroid in the Asteroid Belt. To say the least, it is a lonely and lowly assignment not usually given to officers."

"I see," said Gardener. "Well without any hard evidence of wrongdoing I suppose it is the best that the service can do. It is sufficient for me. I haven't any interest in closing the circle of retribution. Is that all sir?"

"That's all son," said Captain Wingham. "Except I urge you to remain with the mission as long as possible. You are uniquely qualified for this assignment."

"Thank you sir."

Outside the Captain's office, Gardener found Maxine waiting.

"Well?" she said. "What are they going to do about that rat Macland?"

"It's over Maxine," said Gardener.

"What do you mean it's over. After what he did to you."

"I mean it's time to move on."

"Time to move on, is that it? Well Gardener I always said you were crazy for expecting the best out of people and situations and I still say it. But if you're satisfied with the outcome then so am I. I know you well enough to know that your sense of justice has been satisfied even if I don't know how. So what now?"

"Well the corporate board has rewarded me for finishing the mission successfully and offered me whatever I want to stay with the company. I can stay here as lead pilot or I can return to Mars as head of pilot training school."

"So which is it?" asked Maxine impatiently.

"Well I always wanted to fly," said Gardener with a smile.

ABOUT THE AUTHOR

D.W. Patterson lives in the USA with his beautiful wife Sarah. He studied physics and read classic science fiction in college and then worked for many years as an electronic design engineer.

Now he's trying to write stories like the ones he once loved. See his website dwpatterson.com for more information.

Hard Science Fiction – Old School.

Also By This Author:

The Future Chron Universe:

To date the Future Chron Universe has:

51 Amazon Top 100's

(15 in the Top 10)

In chronological order.

Volume numbers indicate Universe order.

Book numbers indicate Series order.

From The Earth Series

(Novellas except where noted):

Volume 1, Book 1 – *Whatsoever You Do*

Volume 2, Book 2 – *War Through The Pines*

Volume 3, Book 3 – *Vigilance*

Volume 4, Book 4 – *To Tend And Watch Over*

Volume 5, Book 5 – *Union*

Volume 6, Book 6 – *Circle Of Retribution*

Volume 7, Book 7 – *Freedom From Want*

Volume 8, Book 8 – *Break Up*

Volume 9, Book 9 – *Kuiper Station*

Volume 10, Book 10 – *The Cloud*

Volume 11, Book 11 – *First Interstellar* – A Short Novel

Wormhole Series

(Novels):

Volume 12, Book 1 – *Mach's Metric*

Volume 13, Book 2 – *Mach's Mission*

Open Space Series

(Short Stories):

Volume 14, Book 1 – *Open Space*

Volume 15, Book 2 – *The Old World*

Volume 16, Book 3 – *Insurrect*

Volume 17, Book 4 – *Second Beam*

Volume 18, Book 5 – *All For One*

Volume 19, Book 6 – *One For All*

Volume 20, Book 7 – *Shotgun*

Volume 21, Book 8 – *Allison*

To The Stars Series

(Novellas):

Volume 22, Book 1 – *First One Hundred*

Volume 23, Book 2 – *First Dark Ages*

Volume 24, Book 3 – *Second One Hundred*

Volume 25, Book 4 – *Second Dark Ages*

Volume 26, Book 5 – *Path Of The Long March*

Wormhole Series

(Novel):

Volume 27, Book 3 – *Mach's Legacy*

Robot Series

(Novels):

Volume 28, Book 1 – *Spin-Two*

Volume 29, Book 2 – *Robot Planet*

Volume 30, Book 3 – *The Lattice Of Space*

Time Series

(Novels):

Volume 31, Book 1 – *Time Wars*

Volume 32, Book 2 – *Time's End*

Volume 33, Book 3 – *Frozen Time*

The Remembered Earth Universe:

To date the Remembered Earth Universe has:

8 Amazon Top 100's

Cislunar Series

(Short Stories):

Volume 1, Book 1 – *US Tugs*

Volume 2, Book 2 – *Prototype*

Volume 3, Book 3 – *L1 Or Bust*

Volume 4, Book 4 – *Guidance Box*

Volume 5, Book 5 – *Air Brakes*

Volume 6, Book 6 – *View Point*

Volume 7, Book 7 – *Space Truck*

Volume 8, Book 8 – *Dark Side* – *In Progress*

The Manifold Earth Universe:

Volume 1, Book 1 – *The Realm* – *In Progress*

Don't miss out!

Visit the website below and you can sign up to receive emails whenever D.W. Patterson publishes a new book. There's no charge and no obligation.

https://books2read.com/r/B-A-DPWE-JWFJC

BOOKS 2 READ

Connecting independent readers to independent writers.

www.ingramcontent.com/pod-product-compliance
Lightning Source LLC
LaVergne TN
LVHW010502160826
845677LV00012B/2621

* 9 7 9 8 2 2 3 0 4 3 4 0 9 *